For Gemk,

Whose endless supply of ideas and honest critique made this possible.

感謝 Gemk

源源不絕的靈感及誠懇的建議讓這一切成真。

The King Who Knew  Kung Fu

會功夫的國王

Coleen Reddy 著

安 宏 繪

薛慧儀 譯

三民書局

In a beautiful palace, there lived a king.

The king was rich but he was not happy.

The king had a beautiful wife but still he was not happy.

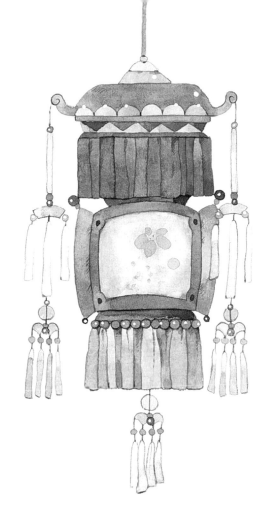

從前有一個國王，住在一座美麗的宮殿裡。
雖然他有很多錢，還有一位漂亮的王后，
但他還是不快樂。

There was something strange about the king.

He was really SHORT.

He was shorter than his wife and all his friends.

He was the shortest person in the palace.

因為國王有一個缺點，
那就是他太矮了。
他比自己的妻子和朋友都矮。
他是宮殿裡最矮的人呢！

The king was afraid.

He was so short.

If a bad person attacked him, what could he do?

He could not fight. What could he do?

He could do nothing. He would die.

國王好害怕喔！

他這麼矮，要是有壞人攻擊他的話，他該怎麼辦呢？

他根本打不過壞人，到時候該怎麼辦才好？

他一點法子都沒有，只有等死了。

But the king did not want to die.
He wanted to learn kung fu.
If anyone attacked him,
he could do kung fu and protect himself.

8

但國王可不想死呀！
所以他想要學功夫。
這樣如果有人攻擊他，
他就可以用功夫來保護自己。

So the short king got a trainer to teach him kung fu.
But sad to say, he was not good at kung fu.
He couldn't kick or hit very well.
In fact, when he did kung fu he looked like
he was doing some kind of crazy dance.

所以矮國王找了一個武術師父來教他功夫。
但說來傷心,他對功夫真是一竅不通呢!
他踢得不高,打得也沒勁兒。
事實上,他練功夫的時候,
看起來就好像在跳一種怪異的舞蹈喔!

11

12

But he WAS the king.

So when he asked, "How was that?" and "Was I good?"

the servants just said, "You were great."

They did not want to tell him the truth. They were afraid to.

不過，他可是一國之君呢！
所以當他問：「剛剛那招怎麼樣？」或「我打得不錯吧？」時，
僕人們也只好說：「您真是棒極了！」他們都不敢把真相告訴國王。

Every time the king practiced his kung fu,
his opponent would pretend to lose.
Then they would say, "Oh king, you are so strong and good at kung fu,
I cannot fight you."
The king thought he really was good at kung fu.

每次國王練功時，他的對手都會假裝被擊倒。
然後他們會說：「喔！陛下！您的武功真是太高強了！
我根本打不過您啊！」
於是國王便以為自己真的是個功夫高手。

The king went on a trip to Australia.

He went to a farm to see the koala bears and kangaroos.

A baby kangaroo stole his keys.

國王去澳洲旅行。
他到農場裡去看無尾熊和袋鼠。
有隻袋鼠寶寶偷走了他的鑰匙。

The king ran after the kangaroo.
The farmer said, "Be careful, those kangaroos can kick very hard."
The king said, "I can do kung fu and I am very good at it. I'll teach that kangaroo a lesson."

國王追著袋鼠寶寶跑。
農夫警告他說：「小心點，這些袋鼠很會踢人的喔！」
國王說：「我有一身好功夫，讓我好好教訓那隻袋鼠！」

The king stood opposite the baby kangaroo.

"Give my keys back to me or I will hurt you," said the king.

The kangaroo giggled.

國王站在袋鼠寶寶面前說：
「把我的鑰匙還給我，不然我可要揍你囉！」
袋鼠寶寶咯咯咯地笑了起來。

The king got so mad.

"Okay!" said the king.

Then he stood in a funny pose with his one leg up in the air and his hands out stretched like he was a bird.

國王好生氣喔！
「好吧！」國王說。
他站成一個滑稽的姿勢，一隻腳騰空，
雙手向兩邊張開，彷彿他是一隻鳥。

"Take THIS!" "Take THAT!" "Hai Ya!"
screamed the king and tried to knock the kangaroo over.
Everyone at the farm started laughing.
The king did not look like a scary kung fu fighter.
He looked like he was playing a game.

「看招！」「來吧！」「嘿！呀！」
國王一面出招一面怪叫，試著把袋鼠寶寶打倒。
農場裡的每個人都笑了起來，
因為國王看起來根本不像個嚇人的武術大師，
倒像是在耍把戲呢！

The kangaroo lifted his leg just once and kicked the king.

It did not kick hard but the king fell down.

He was so embarrassed.

A baby kangaroo had beaten him.

袋鼠寶寶舉起腳來，一下子就踢中了國王！
其實牠踢得並不是很用力，但國王卻應聲而倒。
國王覺得真尷尬。
他竟然被一隻袋鼠寶寶打倒了！

When the king got back home he called all his servants.
"You lied to me," he said. "You told me that I was good at
kung fu but I know that I am not," said the angry king.
He fired all of his servants.

國王回家後，把所有的僕人都叫了過來。
「你們都在說謊！你們都說我武藝高強，
但是我知道我的功夫差得很！」國王生氣地說。
他把所有的僕人都炒魷魚了。

His wife said, "What will you do? Who will protect you?"

"Do not worry about that," said the king. "I have new servants now. They will protect me."

"Who are your new servants?" asked his wife.

"Take a look," said the king, pointing to the garden outside.

There in the garden, were lots of kangaroos practicing kung fu!

王后說：「你以後怎麼辦呢？誰來保護你呢？」

「別擔心，我已經有新的僕人囉！他們會保護我的。」國王說。

「你的新僕人是誰呀？」他的妻子問。

「看看那邊。」國王指指外面的花園。

在花園裡，有好多好多的袋鼠正在練功夫呢！

看圖學單字

小朋友，在玩這個遊戲之前，請先按下 track 3，聽一遍右頁所附的字彙，也可以請爸爸媽媽陪你一起聽、一起念。單字記好了之後，就可以按下 track 4，然後你會聽到下面故事中文的部分，但是遇到有圖的地方，就要由你來把圖片代表的英文單字大聲地喊出來（記得要很大聲喔！）。看看你都會了嗎？

從前有一個 ，他有一位漂亮的 ，他喜歡打 ，

好保護他自己。但是他身材很矮小，所以 打不好。

有天他到澳洲去，看到許多 和 ，

有一隻 baby 偷了他的  ，讓他非常地生氣。

於是，這個 就用 和那隻 打了起來，

那隻 踢了這個 一腳，結果 就飛了出去。

哎呀呀！好痛！

最後，可以按下 track 5，讓我們大家一起來，把這個故事再念一次。

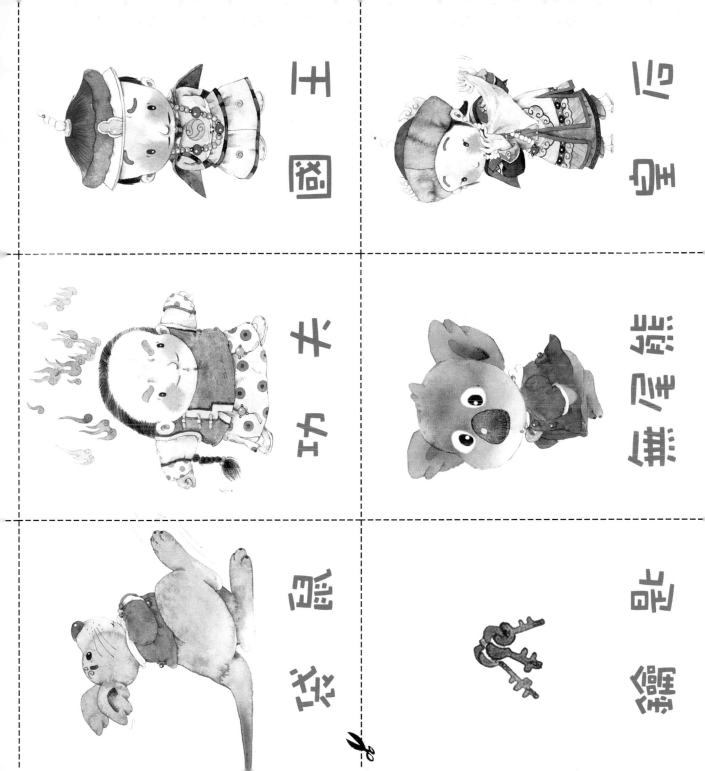

王國

女皇

王子

無尾熊

企鵝

鑰匙

king

queen

kung fu

koala bear

kangaroo

key

生字表

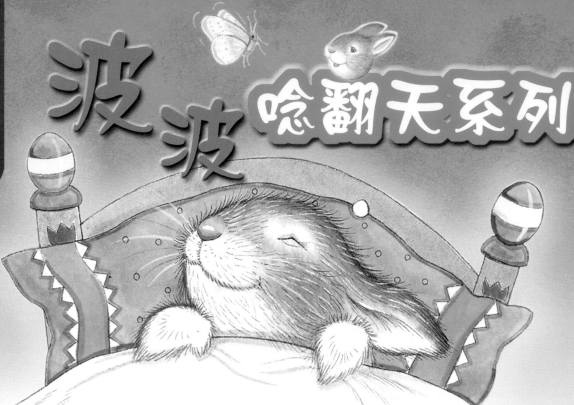

中高級‧中英對照
探索英文叢書

波波唸翻天系列

你知道可愛的小兔子也會 "碎碎唸" 嗎？
波波就是這樣。
他將要告訴我們什麼有趣的故事呢？

波波的復活節／波波的西部冒險記／波波上課記／我愛你，波波
波波的下雪天／波波郊遊去／波波打球記／聖誕快樂，波波／波波的萬聖夜

共 9 本，每本均附 CD

國家圖書館出版品預行編目資料

The King Who Knew Kung Fu:會功夫的國王 /
Coleen Reddy著; 安宏繪; 薛慧儀譯.－－初版一
刷.－－臺北市; 三民, 2003
　　面; 　公分－－(愛閱雙語叢書.二十六個妙朋
友系列) 中英對照
ISBN 957－14－3768－9 　(精裝)

1.英國語言－讀本

523.38　　　　　　　　　　　　　　92008809

© **The King Who Knew Kung Fu**
　　　—— 會功夫的國王

著作人	Coleen Reddy
繪　圖	安　宏
譯　者	薛慧儀
發行人	劉振強
著作財產權人	三民書局股份有限公司 臺北市復興北路386號
發行所	三民書局股份有限公司 地址 / 臺北市復興北路386號 電話 / (02)25006600 郵撥 / 0009998－5
印刷所	三民書局股份有限公司
門市部	復北店 / 臺北市復興北路386號 重南店 / 臺北市重慶南路一段61號

初版一刷　2003年7月
　編　號　S 85644－1
　定　價　新臺幣壹佰捌拾元整
行政院新聞局登記證局版臺業字第○二○○號

ISBN　957－14－3768－9　　(精裝)